THIS IGLOO BOOK BELONGS TO:

....

igloobooks

Published in 2017
by Igloo Books Ltd
Cottage Farm
Sywell
NN6 0BJ
www.igloobooks.com

REX001 0517
2 4 6 8 10 9 7 5 3 1
ISBN 978-1-78670-649-2

Illustrated by David Creighton-Pester
Written by Melanie Joyce

Cover Designed by Nicholas Gage
Interiors designed by Amy Bradford
Edited by Hannah Cather

Printed and manufactured in China

WHO'S AFRAID OF THE DARK?

igloobooks

If you go into the dark
and tiptoe about at night,
nothing will look the same
as it does when it is light.

The sun will sink from the sky
and the moon will shine fat and round.

Shapes will creep from the
wood and STRETCH
along the ground.

But there's no need to worry,
or for you to be afraid.
The shapes are only shadows
that the branches of trees have made.
It's true, the dark is full of things that
CREAK and CRACK and MOAN.

Things that JUMP,
things that go BUMP,
and things that
GRUMBLE and GROAN.

But you'll find it's just a badger, MUNCHING on a midnight snack,
SHUFFLING over twigs and sticks along the forest track.

Perhaps he'll stop for a chat
or play a game or two.
Then he'll be on his way,
wave goodbye and say,
"THANK YOU!"

If you do go into the dark,

always remember to look behind,

because lurking in the shadows,

who knows what you might find?

Bats could fly out of the trees

and get tangled in your hair,

or suddenly you'll hear a

SNAP and ask...

... "IS ANYBODY THERE?"

It will only be the night owl
SWOOPING through the sky.
"HOO-HOO!" he'll say to you,
as he goes flying by.

The fluffy owlets in the nest might sing a song for you.
They'll flap their little wings and go, "TE-WIT, TE-WIT, TE-WOO!"

But are there really monsters hiding in places you can't see?

And do you think to yourself,

"ARE THEY FOLLOWING ME?"

Don't worry, it's only the hedgehogs, SHUFFLING by the wall,

making their way back to their house, and not monsters after all.

If you go out into the dark
and miss the daytime sun...

... remember that playing in the
moonlight can really be lots of fun.

You can SPLASH in glittery pools
and watch the little fish.
If a shooting star ZOOMS by,
then you can make a magic wish.

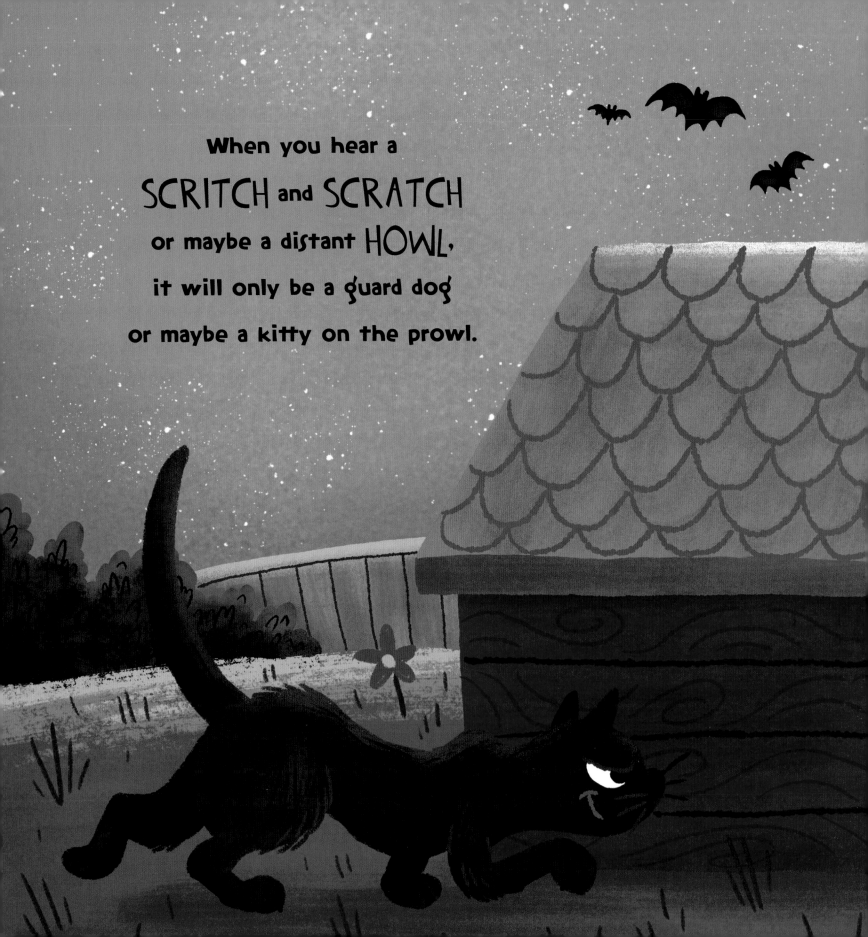

When you hear a
SCRITCH and SCRATCH
or maybe a distant HOWL,
it will only be a guard dog
or maybe a kitty on the prowl.

You will hear noises at night
and wonder what they could be.
It doesn't mean they're scary,
just because you can't see.

So if you're afraid of the dark
and think you should beware,
remember that you're not alone and
someone will always be there.

You'll get a hug and a kiss,

and maybe a story, too.

Then you'll yawn and know that

it really is bedtime for you.

You'll just curl up, safe and warm,
in the glow of the light.

And think of all the things
that you saw in the night.
You might hear a SNAP,
a HOOT, a CRACK, or a BARK,
but you'll know just what it is
and won't be afraid of the dark.